Jacob and Wilhelm

Grimm

Tom Thumb and Other Fairy Tales

PENGUIN BOOKS

PENGUIN BOOKS

Published by the Penguin Group
Penguin Books Ltd, 27 Wrights Lane, London W8 5TZ, England
Penguin Books USA Inc., 375 Hudson Street, New York, New York 10014, USA
Penguin Books Australia Ltd, Ringwood, Victoria, Australia
Penguin Books Canada Ltd, 10 Alcorn Avenue, Toronto, Ontario, Canada M4V 3B2
Penguin Books (NZ) Ltd, 182–190 Wairau Road, Auckland 10, New Zealand

Penguin Books Ltd, Registered Offices: Harmondsworth, Middlesex, England

First published in *Grimms' Fairy Tales* 1923
Published in Puffin Books 1948

This collection published in Penguin Books 1996
1 3 5 7 9 10 8 6 4 2

Set in 12.5/14.5pt Bembo Monotype
Typeset by Datix International Limited, Bungay, Suffolk
Printed in England by Clays Ltd, St Ives plc

Contents

The Twelve Dancing Princesses

THERE was a king who had twelve beautiful daughters. They slept in twelve beds all in one room; and when they went to bed, the doors were shut and locked up; but every morning their shoes were found to be quite worn through as if they had been danced in all night; and yet nobody could find out how it happened, or where they had been.

Then the king made it known to all the land, that if any person could discover the secret, and find out where it was that the princesses danced in the night, he should have the one he liked best for his wife, and should be king after his death; but whoever tried and did not succeed, after three days and nights, should be put to death.

A king's son soon came. He was well entertained, and in the evening was taken to the chamber next to the one where the princesses lay in their twelve beds. There he was to sit and watch where they went to dance; and, in order that nothing might pass without his hearing it, the door of his chamber was left open. But the king's son soon fell asleep; and when he awoke in the morning he found that the princesses had all been dancing, for the soles of their shoes were full of holes. The same thing happened the second and third night: so the king ordered his head to be cut off. After him came several others; but they had all the same luck, and all lost their lives in the same manner.

Now it chanced that an old soldier, who had been wounded in battle and could fight no longer, passed through the country where this king reigned: and as he was travelling through a wood, he met an old woman, who asked him where he was going. 'I hardly know where I am going, or what I had better do,' said the soldier; 'but I think I should like very well to find out where it is that the princesses dance, and then in time I might be a king.' 'Well,' said the old dame, 'that is no very hard task: only take care not to
 drink any of the wine which one of the prin-

cesses will bring to you in the evening; and as soon as she leaves you pretend to be fast asleep.'

Then she gave him a cloak, and said, 'As soon as you put that on you will become invisible, and you will then be able to follow the princesses wherever they go.' When the soldier heard all this good counsel, he determined to try his luck: so he went to the king, and said he was willing to undertake the task.

He was as well received as the others had been, and the king ordered fine royal robes to be given him; and when the evening came he was led to the outer chamber. Just as he was going to lie down, the eldest of the princesses brought him a cup of wine; but the soldier threw it all away secretly, taking care not to drink a drop. Then he laid himself down on his bed, and in a little while began to snore very loud as if he was fast asleep. When the twelve princesses heard this they laughed heartily; and the eldest said, 'This fellow too might have done a wiser thing than lose his life in this way!' Then they rose up and opened their drawers and boxes, and took out all their fine clothes, and dressed themselves at the glass, and skipped about as if they were eager to begin dancing. But the youngest said, 'I don't know how it is, while you are so happy I feel very uneasy; I am sure some mischance will befall us.' 'You simpleton,' said the eldest, 'you are always afraid; have you forgotten how many kings' sons have already watched us in vain? And as for this soldier, even if I had not given him his sleeping draught, he would have slept soundly enough.'

When they were all ready, they went and looked at the soldier; but he snored on, and did not stir hand or foot: so they thought they were quite safe; and the eldest went up to her own bed and clapped her hands, and the bed sunk into the floor and a trap-door flew open. The soldier saw them going down through the trap-door one after another, the eldest leading the way; and thinking he had no time to lose, he jumped up, put on the cloak which the old woman had given him, and followed them; but in the middle of the stairs he trod on the gown of the youngest princess, and she cried out to her sisters, ‘All is not right; some one took hold of my gown.’ ‘You silly creature!’ said the eldest, ‘it is nothing but a nail in the wall.’ Then down they all went, and at the bottom they found themselves in a most delightful grove of trees; and the leaves were all of silver, and glittered and sparkled beautifully. The soldier wished to take away some token of the place; so he broke off a little branch, and there came a loud noise from the tree. Then the youngest daughter said again, ‘I am sure all is not right – did not you hear that noise? That never happened before.’ But the eldest said, ‘It is only our princes, who are shouting for joy at our approach.’

Then they came to another grove of trees, where all the leaves were of gold; and afterwards to a third, where the leaves were all glittering diamonds. And the soldier broke a branch from each; and every time there was a loud noise, which made the youngest sister tremble with fear; but the eldest still said, It was only the princes, who were crying for joy. So they went on till they came to a great lake; and at the side of the lake there lay twelve little boats with twelve handsome princes in them, who seemed to be waiting there for the princesses.

One of the princesses went into each boat, and the soldier stepped into the same boat with the youngest. As they were rowing over the lake, the prince who was in the boat with the youngest princess and the soldier said, 'I do not know why it is, but though I am rowing with all my might we do not get on so fast as usual, and I am quite tired: the boat seems very heavy to-day.' 'It is only the heat of the weather,' said the princess 'I feel it very warm too.'

On the other side of the lake stood a fine illuminated castle, from which came the merry music of horns and trumpets. There they all landed, and went into the castle, and each prince danced with his princess; and the soldier, who was all the time invisible, danced with them too; and when any of the princesses had a cup of wine set by her, he drank it all up, so that when she put the cup to her mouth it was empty. At this, too, the youngest sister was terribly frightened, but the eldest always silenced her. They danced on till three o'clock in the morning, and then all their shoes were worn out, so that they were obliged to leave off. The princes rowed them back again over the lake; (but this time the soldier placed himself in the boat with the eldest princess;) and on the opposite shore they took leave of each other, the princesses promising to come again the next night.

When they came to the stairs, the soldier ran on before the princesses, and laid himself down; and as the twelve sisters slowly came up very much tired, they heard him snoring in his bed; so they said, 'Now all is quite safe;' then they undressed themselves, put away their fine clothes, pulled off their shoes, and went to bed. In the morning the soldier said nothing about what had happened, but determined to see more of this strange adventure, and went again the second and third night; and every thing happened just as before; the princesses danced each time till their shoes were worn to pieces, and then returned home. However, on the third night the soldier carried away one of the golden cups as a token of where he had been.

As soon as the time came when he was to declare the secret, he was taken before the king with the three branches and the golden cup; and the twelve princesses stood listening behind the door to hear what he would say. And when the king asked him. 'Where do my twelve daughters dance at night?' he answered, 'With twelve princes in a castle under ground.' And then he told the king all that had happened, and showed him the three branches and the golden cup which he had brought with him. Then the king called for the princesses, and asked them whether what the soldier said was true: and when they saw that they were discovered, and that it was of no use to deny what had happened, they confessed it all. And the king asked the soldier which of them he would choose for his wife; and he answered, 'I am not very young, so I will have the eldest.' – And they were married that very day, and the soldier was chosen to be the king's heir.

Tom Thumb

THERE was once a poor woodman sitting by the fire in his cottage, and his wife sat by his side spinning. 'How lonely it is,' said he, 'for you and me to sit here by ourselves without any children to play about and amuse us, while other people seem so happy and merry with their children!' 'What you say is very true,' said the wife, sighing and turning round her wheel, 'how happy should I be if I had but one child! and if it were ever so small, nay, if it were no bigger than my thumb, I should be very happy, and love it dearly.' Now it came to pass that this good woman's wish was fulfilled just as she desired; for, some time afterwards, she had a little boy who was quite healthy and strong, but not much bigger than my thumb. So they said, 'Well, we cannot say we have not got what we wished for, and, little as he is, we all love him dearly;' and they called him Tom Thumb.

 They gave him plenty of food, yet he never

grew bigger, but remained just the same size as when he was born; still his eyes were sharp and sparkling, and he soon showed himself to be a clever little fellow, who always knew well what he was about. One day, as the woodman was getting ready to go into the wood to cut fuel, he said, 'I wish I had some one to bring the cart after me, for I want to make haste.' 'O father!' cried Tom, 'I will take care of that; the cart shall be in the wood by the time you want it.' Then the woodman laughed, and said, 'How can that be? you cannot reach up to the horse's bridle.' 'Never mind that, father,' said Tom; 'if my mother will only harness the horse, I will get into his ear and tell him which way to go.' 'Well,' said the father, 'we will try for once.'

When the time came, the mother harnessed the horse to the cart, and put Tom into his ear; and as he sat there, the little man told the beast how to go, crying out, 'Go on,' and 'Stop,' as he wanted; so the horse went on just as if the woodman had driven it himself into the wood. It happened that, as the horse was going a little too fast, and Tom was calling out 'Gently! gently!' two strangers came up. 'What an odd thing that is!' said one, 'there is a cart going along, and I hear a carter talking to the horse, but can see no one.' 'That is strange,' said the other; 'let us follow the cart and see where it goes.' So they went on into the wood, till at last they came to the place where the woodman was. Then Tom Thumb, seeing his father, cried out, 'See, father, here I am, with the cart, all right and safe; now take me down.' So his father took hold of the horse with one hand, and with the other took his son out of the ear; then he put him down upon a straw, where he sat as merry as you please. The two strangers were all this time looking on, and did not know what to say for wonder. At last one took the other aside and said, 'That little urchin will make our fortune if we can get him and carry him about from town to town as a show: we must buy him.' So they went to the woodman and asked him what he would take for the little man: 'He will be better off,' said

 they, 'with us than with you.' 'I won't sell him at

all,' said the father, 'my own flesh and blood is dearer to me than all the silver and gold in the world.' But Tom, hearing of the bargain they wanted to make, crept up his father's coat to his shoulder, and whispered in his ear, 'Take the money, father, and let them have me, I'll soon come back to you.'

So the woodman at last agreed to sell Tom to the strangers for a large piece of gold. 'Where do you like to sit?' said one of them. 'Oh! put me on the rim of your hat, that will be a nice gallery for me; I can walk about there, and see the country as we go along.' So they did as he wished; and when Tom had taken leave of his father, they took him away with them. They journeyed on till it began to be dusky, and then the little man said, 'Let me get down, I'm tired.' So the man took off his hat and set him down on a clod of earth in a ploughed field by the side of the road. But Tom ran about amongst the furrows, and at last slipt into an old mouse-hole. 'Good night, masters,' said he, 'I'm off! mind and look sharp after me the next time.' They ran directly to the place, and poked the ends of their sticks into the mouse-hole, but all in vain; Tom only crawled farther and farther in, and at last it became quite dark, so that they were obliged to go their way without their prize, as sulky as you please.

When Tom found they were gone, he came out of his hiding-place. 'What dangerous walking it is,' said he, 'in this ploughed field! If I were to fall from one of these great clods, I should certainly break my neck.' At last, by good luck, he found a large empty snail-shell. 'This is lucky,' said he, 'I can sleep here very well,' and in he crept. Just as he was falling asleep he heard two men passing, and one said to the other, 'How shall we manage to steal that rich parson's silver and gold?' 'I'll tell you,' cried Tom. 'What noise was that?' said the thief, frightened, 'I am sure I heard some one speak.' They stood still listening, and Tom said, 'Take me with you, and I'll soon show you how to get the parson's money.' 'But where are you?' said they. 'Look
 about on the ground,' answered he, 'and listen

where the sound comes from.' At last the thieves found him out, and lifted him up in their hands. 'You little urchin!' said they, 'what can you do for us?' 'Why I can get between the iron window-bars of the parson's house, and throw you out whatever you want.' 'That's a good thought,' said the thieves, 'come along, we shall see what you can do.'

When they came to the parson's house, Tom slipt through the window-bars into the room, and then called out as loud as he could bawl, 'Will you have all that is here?' At this the thieves were frightened, and said, 'Softly, softly! Speak low, that you may not awaken any body.' But Tom pretended not to understand them, and bawled out again, 'How much will you have? Shall I throw it all out?' Now the cook lay in the next room, and hearing a noise she raised herself in her bed and listened. Meantime the thieves were frightened, and ran off to a little distance; but at last they plucked up courage, and said, 'The little urchin is only trying to make fools of us.' So they came back and whispered softly to him, saying, 'Now let us have no more of your jokes, but throw out some of the money.' Then Tom called out as loud as he could, 'Very well: hold your hands, here it comes.' The cook heard this quite plain, so she sprang out of bed and ran to open the door. The thieves ran off as if a wolf was at their tails; and the maid, having groped about and found nothing, went away for a light. By the time she returned, Tom had slipt off into the barn; and when the cook had looked about and searched every hole and corner, and found nobody, she went to bed, thinking she must have been dreaming with her eyes open. The little man crawled about in the hay-loft, and at last found a glorious place to finish his night's rest in; so he laid himself down, meaning to sleep till day-light, and then find his way home to his father and mother. But, alas! how cruelly was he disappointed! what crosses and sorrows happen in this world! The cook got up early before day-break to feed the cows: she went straight to the hay-loft, and carried away a large bundle of hay with the little man in the middle of it fast asleep.

He still, however, slept on, and did not awake till he found himself in the mouth of the cow, who had taken him up with a mouthful of hay: 'Good lack-a-day!' said he, 'how did I manage to tumble into the mill?' But he soon found out where he really was, and was obliged to have all his wits about him in order that he might not get between the cow's teeth, and so be crushed to death. At last down he went into her stomach. 'It is rather dark here,' said he; 'they forgot to build windows in this room to let the sun in: a candle would be no bad thing.'

Though he made the best of his bad luck, he did not like his quarters at all; and the worst of it was, that more and more hay was always coming down, and the space in which he was became smaller and smaller. At last he cried out as loud as he could, 'Don't bring me any more hay! Don't bring me any more hay!' The maid happened to be just then milking the cow, and hearing some one speak and seeing nobody, and yet being quite sure it was the same voice that she had heard in the night, she was so frightened that she fell off her stool and overset the milk-pail. She ran off as fast as she could to her master the parson, and said, 'Sir, sir, the cow is talking!' But the parson said, 'Woman, thou art surely mad!' However, he went with her into the cow-house to see what was the matter. Scarcely had they set their foot on the threshold, when Tom called out, 'Don't bring me any more hay!' Then the parson himself was frightened; and thinking the cow was surely bewitched, ordered that she should be killed directly. So the cow was killed, and the stomach, in which Tom lay, was thrown out upon a dunghill.

Tom soon set himself to work to get out, which was not a very easy task; but at last, just as he had made room to get his head out, a new misfortune befell him: a hungry wolf sprang out, and swallowed the whole stomach with Tom in it at a single gulp, and ran away. Tom, however, was not disheartened; and, thinking the wolf would not dislike having some chat with him as he was going along, he called out, 'My good friend, I can show you a famous treat.' 'Where's that?' said the wolf. 'In such and such a house,' said Tom, describing his father's house, 'you can crawl through the drain into the kitchen, and there you will find cakes, ham, beef, and every thing your heart can desire.' The wolf did not want to be asked twice; so that very night he went to the house and crawled through the drain into the kitchen, and ate and drank there to his heart's content. As soon as he was satisfied, he wanted to get away, but he had eaten so much that he could not get out the same way that he came in. This was just what Tom had reckoned upon; and he now began to set up a great shout, making all the noise he could. 'Will you be quiet?' said the wolf: 'you'll awaken every body in the house.' 'What's that to me?' said the little man: 'you have had your frolic, now I've a mind to be merry myself;' and he began again singing and shouting as loud as he could.

The woodman and his wife, being awakened by the noise, peeped through a crack in the door; but when they saw that the wolf was there, you may well suppose that they were terribly frightened; and the woodman ran for his axe, and gave his wife a scythe. – 'Now do you stay behind,' said the woodman 'and when I have knocked him on the head, do you rip up his belly for him with the scythe.' Tom heard all this, and said, 'Father, father! I am here, the wolf has swallowed me:' and his father said, 'Heaven be praised! we have found our dear child again;' and he told his wife not to use the scythe, for fear she should hurt him. Then he aimed a great blow, and struck the wolf on the head, and killed him on the spot; and when he was dead they cut open his body and set Tommy free. 'Ah!' said the father, 'what fears we have had for you!' 'Yes, father,' answered he, 'I have travelled all over the world, since we parted, in one way or other and now I am very glad to get fresh air again.' 'Why, where have you been?' said his father. 'I have been in a mouse-hole, in a snail-shell; down a cow's throat, and in the wolf's belly; and yet here I am again safe and sound.' 'Well,' said they 'we will not sell you again for all the riches in the world.' So they hugged and kissed their dear little son, and gave him plenty to eat and drink, and fetched new clothes for him, for his old ones were quite spoiled on his journey.

The Golden Goose

THERE was a man who had three sons. The youngest was called Dummling, and was on all occasions despised and ill-treated by the whole family. It happened that the eldest took it into his head one day to go into the wood to cut fuel; and his mother gave him a delicious pasty and a bottle of wine to take with him, that he might refresh himself at his work. As he went into the wood, a little old man bid him good day, and said, 'Give me a little piece of meat from your plate, and a little wine out of your bottle; I am very hungry and thirsty.' But this clever young man said, 'Give you my meat and wine! No, I thank you; I should not have enough left for myself:' and away he went. He soon began to cut down a tree; but he had not worked long before he missed his stroke, and cut himself, and was obliged to go home to have the wound dressed. Now it was the little old man that caused him this mischief.

Next went out the second son to work; and his mother gave him too a pasty and a bottle of wine. And the same little old man met him also, and asked him for something to eat and drink. But he too thought himself vastly clever, and said, 'Whatever you get, I shall lose; so go your way!' The little man took care that he should have his reward; and the second stroke that he aimed against a tree, hit him on the leg; so that he too was forced to go home.

Then Dummling said, 'Father, I should like to go and cut wood too.' But his father answered, 'Your brothers have both lamed themselves; you had better stay at home, for you know nothing of the business.' But Dummling was very pressing; and at last his father said, 'Go your way; you will be wiser when you have suffered for your folly.' And his mother gave him only some dry bread, and a bottle of sour beer; but when he went into the wood, he met the little old man, who said, 'Give me some meat and drink, for I am very hungry and thirsty.' Dummling said, 'I have only dry bread and sour beer; if that will suit you, we will sit down and eat it together.' So they sat down; and when the lad pulled out his bread, behold it was turned into a capital pasty, and his sour beer became delightful wine. They ate and drank heartily; and when they had done, the little man said, 'As you have a kind heart, and have been willing to share every thing with me, I will send a blessing upon you. There stands an old tree; cut it down, and you will find something at the root.' Then he took his leave, and went his way.

Dummling set to work, and cut down the tree; and when it fell, he found in a hollow under the roots a goose with feathers of pure gold. He took it up, and went on to an inn, where he proposed to sleep for the night. The landlord had three daughters; and when they saw the goose, they were very curious to examine what this wonderful bird could be, and wished very much to pluck one of the feathers out of its tail. At last the eldest said, 'I must and will have a feather.' So she waited till his back was turned, and then seized the goose by the wing; but to her great surprise there she stuck, for neither hand nor finger could she get away again. Presently in came the second sister, and thought to have a feather too; but the moment she touched her sister, there she too hung fast. At last came the third, and wanted a feather; but the other two cried out, 'Keep away! for heaven's sake, keep away!' However, she did not understand what they meant. 'If they are there,' thought she, 'I may as well be there too.' So she went up to them; but the moment she touched her sisters she stuck fast, and hung to the goose as they did. And so they kept company with the goose all night.

The next morning Dummling carried off the goose under his arm; and took no notice of the three girls, but went out with them sticking fast behind; and wherever he travelled, they too were obliged to follow, whether they would or no, as fast as their legs could carry them.

In the middle of a field the parson met them; and when he saw the train, he said, 'Are you not ashamed of yourselves, you bold girls, to run after the young man in that way over the fields? is that proper behaviour?' Then he took the youngest by the hand to lead her away; but the moment he touched her he too hung fast, and followed in the train. Presently up came the clerk; and when he saw his master the parson running after the three girls, he wondered greatly, and said, 'Hollo! hollo! your reverence! whither so fast? there is a christening to-day.' Then he ran up, and took him by the gown, and in a moment he was fast too. As the five were thus trudging along, one behind another, they met two labourers with their mattocks coming from work; and the parson cried out to them to set him free. But scarcely had they touched him, when they too fell into the ranks, and so made seven, all running after Dummling and his goose.

At last they arrived at a city, where reigned a king who had an only daughter. The princess was of so thoughtful and serious a turn of mind that no one could make her laugh; and the king had proclaimed to all the world, that whoever could make her laugh should have her for his wife. When the young man heard this, he went to her with his goose and all its train; and as soon as she saw the seven all hanging together, and running about, treading on each other's heels she could not help bursting into a long and loud laugh. Then Dummling claimed her for his wife; the wedding was celebrated, and he was heir to the kingdom, and lived long and happily with his wife.

Rumpel-Stilts-Kin

In a certain kingdom once lived a poor miller who had a very beautiful daughter. She was moreover exceedingly shrewd and clever; and the miller was so vain and proud of her, that he one day told the king of the land that his daughter could spin gold out of straw. Now this king was very fond of money; and when he heard the miller's boast, his avarice was excited, and he ordered the girl to be brought before him. Then he led her to a chamber where there was a great quantity of straw, gave her a spinning-wheel, and said, 'All this must be spun into gold before morning, as you value your life.' It was in vain that the poor maiden declared that she could do no such thing, the chamber was locked and she remained alone.

She sat down in one corner of the room and began to lament over her hard fate, when on a sudden the door opened, and a droll-looking little man hobbled in, and said, 'Good morrow to you, my good lass, what are you weeping for?' 'Alas!' answered she, 'I must spin this straw into gold, and I know not how.' 'What will you give me,' said the little man, 'to do it for you?' 'My necklace,' replied the maiden. He took her at her word, and sat himself down to the wheel; round about it went merrily, and presently the work was done and the gold all spun.

When the king came and saw this, he was greatly astonished and pleased; but his heart grew still more greedy of gain, and he shut up the poor miller's daughter again with a fresh task. Then she knew not what to do, and sat down once more to weep; but the little man presently opened the door, and said, 'What will you give me to do your task?' 'The ring on my finger,' replied she. So her little friend took the ring, and began to work at the wheel, till by the morning all was finished again.

The king was vastly delighted to see all this glittering treasure; but still he was not satisfied, and took the miller's daughter into a yet larger room, and said, 'All this must be spun to-night;

and if you succeed, you shall be my queen.' As soon as she was alone the dwarf came in, and said, 'What will you give me to spin gold for you this third time?' 'I have nothing left,' said she. 'Then promise me,' said the little man, 'your first little child when you are queen.' 'That may never be,' thought the miller's daughter; and as she knew no other way to get her task done, she promised him what he asked, and he spun once more the whole heap of gold. The king came in the morning, and finding all he wanted, married her, and so the miller's daughter really became queen.

At the birth of her first little child the queen rejoiced very much, and forgot the little man and her promise; but one day he came into her chamber and reminded her of it. Then she grieved sorely at her misfortune, and offered him all the treasures of the kingdom in exchange; but in vain, till at last her tears softened him, and he said, 'I will give you three days' grace, and if during that time you tell me my name, you shall keep your child.'

Now the queen lay awake all night, thinking

of all the odd names that she had ever heard, and dispatched messengers all over the land to inquire after new ones. The next day the little man came, and she began with Timothy, Benjamin, Jeremiah, and all the names she could remember; but to all of them he said, 'That's not my name.'

The second day she began with all the comical names she could hear of, Bandy-legs, Hunch-back, Crook-shanks, and so on, but the little gentleman still said to every one of them, 'That's not my name.'

The third day came back one of the messengers, and said, 'I can hear of no one other name; but yesterday, as I was climbing a high hill among the trees of the forest where the fox and the hare bid each other good night, I saw a little hut, and before the hut burnt a fire, and round about the fire danced a funny little man upon one leg, and sung

> 'Merrily the feast I'll make,
> Today I'll brew, to-morrow bake;

Merrily I'll dance and sing,
For next day will a stranger bring:
Little does my lady dream
Rumpel-Stilts-Kin is my name!'

When the queen heard this, she jumped for joy, and as soon as her little visitor came, and said, 'Now, lady, what is my name?' 'Is it John?' asked she. 'No!' 'Is it Tom?' 'No!'

'Can your name be Rumpel-Stilts-Kin?'

'Some witch told you that! Some witch told you that!' cried the little man, and dashed his right foot in a rage so deep into the floor, that he was forced to lay hold of it with both hands to pull it out. Then he made the best of his way off, while every body laughed at him for having had all his trouble for nothing.

The Goose-Girl

An old queen, whose husband had been dead some years, had a beautiful daughter. When she grew up, she was betrothed to a prince who lived a great way off; and as the time drew near for her to be married, she got ready to set off on her journey to his country. Then the queen her mother packed up a great many costly things; jewels, and gold, and silver; trinkets, fine dresses, and in short every thing that became a royal bride; for she loved her child very dearly: and she gave her a waiting-maid to ride with her, and gave her into the bridegroom's hands; and each had a horse for the journey. Now the princess's horse was called Falada, and could speak.

When the time came for them to set out, the old queen went into her bed-chamber, and took a little knife, and cut off a lock of her hair, and gave it to her daughter, and said, 'Take care of it, dear child; for it is a charm that may be of use to you on the road.' Then they took a sorrowful leave of each other, and the princess put the lock of her mother's hair into her bosom, got upon her horse, and set off on her journey to her bridegroom's kingdom. One day, as they were riding along by the side of a brook, the princess began to feel very thirsty, and said to her maid, 'Pray get down and fetch me some water in my golden cup out of yonder brook, for I want to drink.' 'Nay,' said the maid, 'if you are thirsty, get down yourself, and lie down by the water and drink; I shall not be your waiting-maid any longer.' Then she was so thirsty that she got down, and knelt over the little brook, and drank, for she was frightened, and dared not bring out her golden cup; and then she wept, and said, 'Alas! what will become of me?' And the lock of hair answered her, and said,

> 'Alas! alas! if my mother knew it,
> Sadly, sadly her heart would rue it.'

 But the princess was very humble and meek, so

she said nothing to her maid's ill behaviour, but got upon her horse again.

Then all rode farther on their journey, till the day grew so warm, and the sun so scorching, that the bride began to feel very thirsty again; and at last when they came to a river she forgot her maid's rude speech, and said, 'Pray get down and fetch me some water to drink in my golden cup.' But the maid answered her, and even spoke more haughtily than before, 'Drink if you will, but I shall not be your waiting-maid.' Then the princess was so thirsty that she got off her horse, and lay down, and held her head over the running stream, and cried, and said, 'What will become of me?' And the lock of hair answered her again,

> 'Alas! alas! if my mother knew it
> Sadly, sadly her heart would rue it.'

And as she leaned down to drink, the lock of hair fell from her bosom, and floated away with the water, without her seeing it, she was so frightened. But her maid saw it, and was very glad, for she knew the charm, and saw that the poor bride would be in her power, now that she had lost the hair. So when the bride had done, and would have got upon Falada again, the maid said, 'I shall ride upon Falada, and you may have my horse instead:' so she was forced to give up her horse, and soon afterwards to take off her royal clothes, and put on her maid's shabby ones.

At last, as they drew near the end of their journey, this treacherous servant threatened to kill her mistress if she ever told any one what had happened. But Falada saw it all, and marked it well. Then the waiting-maid got upon Falada, and the real bride was set upon the other horse and they went on in this way till at last they came to the royal court. There was great joy at their coming, and the prince flew to meet them, and lifted the maid from her horse, thinking she was the one who was to be his wife; and she was led up stairs to the royal chamber, but the true princess was told to stay in the court below.

But the old king happened to be looking out of the window, and saw her in the yard below;

and as she looked very pretty, and too delicate for a waiting-maid, he went into the royal chamber to ask the bride who it was she had brought with her, that was thus left standing in the court below. 'I brought her with me for the sake of her company on the road,' said she; 'pray give the girl some work to do, that she may not be idle.' The old king could not for some time think of any work for her to do; but at last he said, 'I have a lad who takes care of my geese; she may go and help him.' Now the name of this lad, that the real bride was to help in watching the king's geese, was Curdken.

Soon after, the false bride said to the prince, 'Dear husband, pray do me one piece of kindness.' 'That I will,' said the prince. 'Then tell one of your slaughterers to cut off the head of the horse I rode upon, for it was very unruly, and plagued me sadly on the road:' but the truth was, she was very much afraid lest Falada should speak, and tell all she had done to the princess. She carried her point, and the faithful Falada was killed: but when the true princess heard of it, she wept, and begged the man to nail up Falada's head against a large dark gate of the city, through which she had to pass every morning and evening, that there she might still see him sometimes. Then the slaughterer said he would do as she wished; and cut off the head, and nailed it fast under the dark gate.

Early the next morning, as she and Curdken went out through the gate, she said sorrowfully,

'Falada, Falada, there thou art hanging!'

and the head answered

'Bride, bride, there thou art ganging!
Alas! alas! if thy mother knew it,
Sadly, sadly her heart would rue it.'

Then they went out of the city, and drove the geese on. And when she came to the meadow, she sat down upon a bank there, and let down her waving locks of hair, which were all of pure
 silver; and when Curdken saw it glitter in the

sun, he ran up, and would have pulled some of the locks out; but she cried,

'Blow, breezes, blow!
Let Curdken's hat go!
Blow, breezes, blow!
Let him after it go!
O'er hills, dales, and rocks,
Away be it whirl'd,
Till the silvery locks
Are all comb'd and curl'd!'

Then there came a wind, so strong that it blew off Curdken's hat; and away it flew over the hills, and he after it; till, by the time he came back, she had done combing and curling her hair, and put it up again safe. Then he was very angry and sulky, and would not speak to her at all; but they watched the geese until it grew dark in the evening, and then drove them homewards.

The next morning, as they were going through the dark gate, the poor girl looked up at Falada's head, and cried,

'Falada, Falada, there thou art hanging!'

and it answered

'Bride, bride, there thou art ganging!
Alas! alas! if thy mother knew it,
Sadly, sadly her heart would rue it.'

Then she drove on the geese, and sat down again in the meadow, and began to comb out her hair as before; and Curdken ran up to her, and wanted to take hold of it; but she cried out quickly,

'Blow, breezes, blow!
Let Curdken's hat go!
Blow, breezes, blow!
Let him after it go!
O'er hills, dales, and rocks,
Away be it whirl'd,
Till the silvery locks
Are all comb'd and curl'd!'

Then the wind came and blew his hat, and off it flew a great way, over the hills and far away, so that he had to run after it; and when he came back, she had done up her hair again, and all was safe. So they watched the geese till it grew dark.

In the evening, after they came home, Curdken went to the old king, and said, 'I cannot have that strange girl to help me to keep the geese any longer.' 'Why?' said the king. 'Because she does nothing but tease me all day long.' Then the king made him tell him all that had passed. And Curdken said, 'When we go in the morning through the dark gate with our flock of geese, she weeps, and talks with the head of a horse that hangs upon the wall, and says,

> 'Falada, Falada, there thou art hanging!'

and the head answers,

> 'Bride, bride, there thou art ganging!
> Alas! alas! if thy mother knew it,
> Sadly, sadly her heart would rue it.'

And Curdken went on telling the king what had happened upon the meadow where the geese fed; and how his hat was blown away, and he was forced to run after it, and leave his flock. But the old king told him to go out again as usual the next day; and when morning came, he placed himself behind the dark gate, and heard how she spoke to Falada, and how Falada answered; and then he went into the field, and hid himself in a bush by the meadow's side, and soon saw with his own eyes how they drove the flock of geese, and how, after a little time, she let down her hair that glittered in the sun; and then he heard her say,

'Blow, breezes, blow!
Let Curdken's hat go!
Blow, breezes, blow!
Let him after it go!
O'er hills, dales, and rocks,
Away be it whirl'd,
Till the silvery locks
Are all comb'd and curl'd!'

And soon came a gale of wind, and carried away Curdken's hat, while the girl went on combing and curling her hair. All this the old king saw: so he went home without being seen; and when the little goose-girl came back in the evening, he called her aside, and asked her why she did so; but she burst into tears, and said, 'That I must not tell you or any man, or I shall lose my life.'

But the old king begged so hard, that she had no peace till she had told him all, word for word: and it was very lucky for her that she did so, for the king ordered royal clothes to be put upon her, and gazed on her with wonder she was so beautiful. Then he called his son, and told him that he had only the false bride, for that she was merely a waiting-maid, while the true one stood by. And the young king rejoiced when he saw her beauty, and heard how meek and patient she had been; and, without saying any thing, ordered a great feast to be got ready for all his court. The bridegroom sat at the top, with the false princess on one side, and the true one on the other; but nobody knew her, for she was quite dazzling to their eyes, and was not at all like the little goose-girl, now that she had her brilliant dress.

When they had eaten and drank, and were very merry, the old king told all the story, as one that he had once heard of, and asked the true waiting-maid what she thought ought to be done to any one who would behave thus. 'Nothing better,' said this false bride, 'than that she should be thrown into a cask stuck round with sharp nails, and that two white horses should be put to it, and should drag it from street to street till she is dead.' 'Thou art she!' said the old king, 'and since thou hast judged thyself, it shall be so done to thee.' And the young king was married to his true wife, and they reigned over the kingdom in peace and happiness all their lives.

The Water of Life

LONG before you and I were born there reigned, in a country a great way off, a king who had three sons. This king once fell very ill, so ill that nobody thought he would live. His sons were very much grieved at their father's sickness; and as they walked weeping in the garden of the palace, an old man met them and asked what they ailed. They told him their father was so ill that they were afraid nothing could save him. 'I know what would,' said the old man; 'it is the Water of Life. If he could have a draught of it he would be well again, but it is very hard to get.' Then the eldest son said, 'I will soon find it,' and went to the sick king, and begged that he might go in search of the Water of Life, as it was the only thing that could save him. 'No,' said the king; 'I had rather die than place you in such great danger as you must meet with in your journey.' But he begged so hard that the king let him go; and the prince thought to himself, 'If I bring my father this water I shall be his dearest son, and he will make me heir to his kingdom.'

Then he set out, and when he had gone on his way some time he came to a deep valley overhung with rocks and woods; and as he looked around there stood above him on one of the rocks a little dwarf, who called out to him and said, 'Prince, whither hastest thou so fast?' 'What is that to you, little ugly one?' said the prince sneeringly, and rode on his way. But the little dwarf fell into a great rage at his behaviour, and laid a spell of ill luck upon him, so that, as he rode on, the mountain pass seemed to become narrower and narrower, and at last the way was so straitened that he could not go a step forward, and when he thought to have turned his horse round and gone back the way he came, the passage he found had closed behind also; and shut him quite up; he next tried to get off his horse and make his way on foot, but this he was unable to do, and so there he was forced to abide spell-bound.

 Meantime the king his father was lingering on

in daily hope of his return, till at last the second son said, 'Father, I will go in search of this Water;' for he thought to himself, 'My brother is surely dead, and the kingdom will fall to me if I have good luck in my journey.' The king was at first very unwilling to let him go, but at last yielded to his wish. So he set out and followed the same road which his brother had taken, and met the same dwarf, who stopped him at the same spot, and said as before, 'Prince, whither hastest thou so fast?' 'Mind your own affairs, busy body!' answered the prince scornfully, and rode off. But the dwarf put the same enchantment upon him, and when he came like the other to the narrow pass in the mountains he could neither move forward nor backward. Thus it is with proud silly people, who think themselves too wise to take advice.

When the second prince had thus stayed away a long while, the youngest said he would go and search for the Water of Life, and trusted he should soon be able to make his father well again. The dwarf met him too at the same spot, and said, 'Prince, whither hastest thou so fast?' and the prince said, 'I go in search of the Water of Life, because my father is ill and like to die: – can you help me?' 'Do you know where it is to be found?' asked the dwarf. 'No,' said the prince. 'Then as you have spoken to me kindly and sought for advice, I will tell you how and where to go. The Water you seek springs from a well in an enchanted castle, and that you may be able to go in safety I will give you an iron wand and two little loaves of bread; strike the iron door of the castle three times with the wand, and it will open: two hungry lions will be lying down inside gaping for their prey; but if you throw them the bread they will let you pass; then hasten on to the well and take some of the Water of Life before the clock strikes twelve, for if you tarry longer the door will shut upon you for ever.'

Then the prince thanked the dwarf for his friendly aid, and took the wand and the bread and went travelling on and on over sea and land, till he came to his journey's end, and found every thing to be as the dwarf had told him. The door flew open at the third stroke of the wand, and when the lions were quieted he went on through the castle, and came at length to a beautiful hall; around it he saw several knights sitting in a trance; then he pulled off their rings and put them on his own fingers. In another room he saw on a table a sword and a loaf of bread, which he also took. Farther on he came to a room where a beautiful young lady sat upon a couch, who welcomed him joyfully, and said, if he would set her free from the spell that bound her, the kingdom should be his if he would come back in a year and marry her; then she told him that the well that held the Water of Life was in the palace gardens, and bade him make haste and draw what he wanted before the clock struck twelve. Then he went on, and as he walked through beautiful gardens he came to a delightful shady spot in which stood a couch; and he thought to himself, as he felt tired, that he would rest himself for a while and gaze on the lovely scenes around him. So he laid himself down, and sleep fell upon him unawares and he did not wake up till the clock was striking a quarter to twelve; then he sprung from the couch dreadfully frightened, ran to the well, filled a cup that was standing by him full of Water, and hastened to get away in time. Just as he was going out of the iron door it struck twelve, and the door fell so quickly upon him that it tore away a piece of his heel.

When he found himself safe he was overjoyed to think that he had got the water of Life; and as he was going on his way homewards, he passed by the little dwarf, who when he saw the sword and the loaf said, 'You have made a noble prize; with the sword you can at a blow slay whole armies, and the bread will never fail.' Then the prince thought to himself, 'I cannot go home to my father without my brothers;' so he said, 'Dear dwarf, cannot you tell me where my two brothers are, who set out in search of the Water of Life before me and never came back?' 'I have shut them up by a charm between two mountains,' said the dwarf, 'because they were proud and ill behaved, and scorned to ask advice.' The prince begged so hard for his brothers that the dwarf at last set them free, though unwillingly, saying, 'Beware of them, for they have bad hearts.' Their brother, however, was greatly rejoiced to see them, and told them all that had happened to him, how he had found the Water of Life, and had taken a cup full of it, and how he had set a beautiful princess free from a spell that bound her; and how she had engaged to wait a whole year, and then to marry him and give him the kingdom. Then they all three rode on together, and on their way home came to a country that was laid waste by war and a dreadful famine, so that it was feared all must die for want. But the prince gave the king of the land the bread, and all his kingdom ate of it. And he slew the enemy's army with the wonderful sword, and left the kingdom in peace and plenty. In the same manner he befriended two other countries that they passed through on their way.

When they came to the sea, they got into a ship, and during their voyage the two eldest said to themselves, 'Our brother has got the Water which we could not find, therefore our father will forsake us, and give him the kingdom which is our right;' so they were full of envy and revenge, and agreed together how they could ruin him. They waited till he was fast asleep, and then poured the Water of Life out of the cup and took it for themselves, giving him bitter sea-water instead. And when they came to their journey's end, the youngest son brought his cup to the sick king, that he might drink and be healed. Scarcely, however, had he tasted the bitter sea-water when he became worse even than he was before, and then both the elder sons came in and blamed the youngest for what he had done, and said that he wanted to poison their father, but that they had found the Water of Life and had brought it with them. He no sooner began to drink of what they brought him, than he felt his sickness leave him, and was as strong and well as in his young days; then they went to their brother and laughed at him, and said, 'Well, brother, you found the Water of Life, did you? you have had the trouble and we shall have the reward; pray, with all your cleverness why did not you manage to keep your eyes open? Next year one of us will take away your beautiful princess, if you do not take care; you had better say nothing about this to our father, for he does not believe a word you say, and if you tell tales, you shall lose your life into the bargain, but be quiet and we will let you off.'

The old king was still very angry with his youngest son, and thought he really meant to have taken away his life; so he called his court together and asked what should be done, and it was settled that he should be put to death. The prince knew nothing of what was going on, till one day when the king's chief huntsman went a-hunting with him, and they were alone in the wood together, the huntsman looked so sorrowful that the prince said, 'My friend, what is the matter with you?' 'I cannot and dare not tell you,' said he. But the prince begged hard and said, 'Only say what it is, and do not think I shall be angry, for I will forgive you.' 'Alas!' said the huntsman, 'the king has ordered me to shoot you.' The prince started at this, and said, 'Let me live, and I will change dresses with you; you shall take my royal coat to show to my father, and do you give me your shabby one.' 'With all my heart,' said the huntsman; 'I am sure I shall be glad to save you, for I could not have shot you.' Then he took the prince's coat, and gave him the shabby one, and went away through the wood.

Some time after, three grand embassies came to the old king's court, with rich gifts of gold and precious stones for his youngest son, which were sent from the three kings to whom he had lent his sword and loaf of bread, to rid them of their enemy, and feed their people. This touched the old king's heart, and he thought his son might still be guiltless, and said to his court, 'Oh! that my son were still alive! how it grieves me that I had him killed!' 'He still lives,' said the huntsman; 'and I rejoice that I had pity on him, and saved him, for when the time came, I could not shoot him, but let him go in peace and brought home his royal coat.' At this the king was overwhelmed with joy, and made it known throughout all his kingdom, that if his son would come back to his court, he would forgive him.

Meanwhile the princess was eagerly waiting the return of her deliverer, and had a road made leading up to her palace all of shining gold; and told her courtiers that whoever came on horse-back and rode straight up to the gate upon it, was her true lover, and that they must let him in; but whoever rode on one side of it, they must be sure was not the right one, and must send him away at once.

The time soon came, when the eldest thought he would make haste to go to the princess, and say that he was the one who had set her free, and that he should have her for his wife, and the kingdom with her. As he came before the palace and saw the golden road, he stopt to look at it, and thought to himself, 'It is a pity to ride upon this beautiful road;' so he turned aside and rode on the right of it. But when he came to the gate, the guards said to him, he was not what he said he was, and must go about his business. The second prince set out soon afterwards on the same errand; and when he came to the golden road, and his horse had set one foot upon it, he stopt to look at it, and thought it very beautiful, and said to himself, 'What a pity it is that any thing should tread here!' then he too turned aside and rode on the left of it. But when he came to the gate the guards said he was not the true prince, and that he too must go away.

Now when the full year was come, the third brother left the wood, where he had laid for fear of his father's anger, and set out in search of his betrothed bride. So he journeyed on, thinking of her all the way, and rode so quickly that he did not even see the golden road, but went with his horse straight over it; and as he came to the gate, it flew open, and the princess welcomed him with joy, and said he was her deliverer and should now be her husband and lord of the kingdom, and the marriage was soon kept with great feasting. When it was over, the princess told him she had heard of his father having forgiven him, and of his wish to have him home again: so he went to visit him, and told him every thing, how his brothers had cheated and robbed him, and yet that he had borne all these wrongs for the love of his father. Then the old king was very angry, and wanted to punish his wicked sons; but they made their escape, and got into a ship and sailed away over the wide sea, and were never heard of any more.

Penguin Children's 60s

ALI BABA AND THE FORTY THIEVES • *Retold by N. J. Dawood*
THE AMAZING PIPPI LONGSTOCKING • *Astrid Lindgren*
ANNE AT GREEN GABLES • *L. M. Montgomery*
AT THE RIVER-GATES AND
OTHER SUPERNATURAL STORIES • *Philippa Pearce*
CLASSIC GHOST STORIES
CLASSIC NONSENSE VERSE
THE CLOCKWORK MOUSE • *Dick King-Smith*
DEAD MAN'S LANE • *Joan Aiken*
THE DRAGON ON THE ROOF • *Terry Jones*
FOUR GREAT GREEK MYTHS • *Roger Lancelyn Green*
THE GREAT MOUSE PLOT AND
OTHER TALES OF CHILDHOOD • *Roald Dahl*
THE GREAT TIME WARP ADVENTURE • *Jon Scieszka*
THE HOOLIGAN'S SHAMPOO • *Philip Ridley*
KEEP IT IN THE FAMILY • *Anne Fine*
KING ARTHUR'S COURT • *Roger Lancelyn Green*
THE LITTLE MERMAID AND
OTHER FAIRY TALES • *Hans Andersen (Translated by Naomi Lewis)*
LOST DOG AND OTHER STORIES • *Penelope Lively*
THE MIDNIGHT STORY • *Margaret Mahy*
MOOMINTROLLS AND FRIENDS • *Tove Jansson*
MRS PEPPERPOT TURNS DETECTIVE • *Alf Prøysen*
THE NIGHT TRAIN: STORIES IN PROSE AND VERSE • *Allan Ahlberg*
THE PIED PIPER OF HAMELIN AND OTHER CLASSIC STORIES IN VERSE
ROBIN HOOD AND HIS MERRY MEN • *Roger Lancelyn Green*
SHERLOCK HOLMES AND THE SPECKLED BAND • *Sir Arthur Conan Doyle*
SMACKING MY LIPS • *Michael Rosen*
TALES FROM ALICE IN WONDERLAND • *Lewis Carroll*
TALES FROM THE JUNGLE BOOK • *Rudyard Kipling*
THREE QUIRKY TAILS • *Paul Jennings*
TOM SAWYER'S PIRATE ADVENTURE • *Mark Twain*
TOM THUMB AND OTHER FAIRY TALES • *Jacob and Wilhelm Grimm*

Some other books available from Penguin in Puffin Classics

ALICE'S ADVENTURES IN WONDERLAND • *Lewis Carroll*
A CHRISTMAS CAROL • *Charles Dickens*
HANS ANDERSEN'S FAIRY TALES • *Translated by Naomi Lewis*
THE MYTHS OF THE NORSEMEN • *Roger Lancelyn Green*
TALES OF MYSTERY AND TERROR • *Edgar Allan Poe*